BLACKIE BLEWITT

The Young Harvester Series also includes:

THE GRANDFATHER CLOCK

LIZZIE'S GREAT ESCAPE

PEDRO'S HOLIDAY

ISBN: 1 872547 56 7

Text by Anne Hughson ©1993
Illustrated by Mary Lonsdale © 1993

Set in 13/20 New Century Schoolbook

Published by Sherbourne Publications
Sweeney Mountain, Oswestry
Shropshire SY10 9EX, UK
Tel: 0691 657853

Typesetting by Graphics Services, Aston University
Tel: 021 359 3611

Printed by Welshpool Printing Company (1992) Ltd
Canal Yard, Severn Street, Welshpool, SY21 7AQ
Tel: 0938 552260

For Casca and Benjy

BLACKIE BLEWITT

by

Anne Hughson

Illustrated by Mary Lonsdale

Sherbourne Publications

CHAPTER ONE

Danny bent to stroke the sleek, shining fur of Blackie Blewitt. The fat black cat was always sitting at old Mrs Blewitt's gate when Danny passed on his way home from school. The cat purred. Danny noticed the faded net curtain twitch behind the struggling geraniums on the window sill, and knew the old lady was watching him.

Danny ran into his own house calling, "Mum! Mum!" wanting to tell her about his day. He came to a sudden halt when he found Dad in the kitchen.

His father grinned.

"Don't look so shocked, son. Mum has had to go and stay with Gran for a few days. Gran has had a fall and needs a bit of looking after."

Danny stared in silence, absorbing this unexpected news.

"I'll need your help, Danny," Dad was saying.

"Go and wash your hands and lay the table."

A smile spread across Danny's face and ended in a loud "Whoopee!" as Danny jumped into the air, his fair curly hair becoming more tousled than usual.

"This could be fun!" Danny thought as he turned on the kitchen taps.

As they enjoyed their tea of pie and baked beans Dad announced, "I'm going to drive over to Gran's this evening, and check that Mum can manage everything."

"I'll come," Danny put in eagerly.

"It will be too late for you, Danny. I'll put you to bed, and old Mrs Blewitt is coming to sit in."

"Oh not her, Dad," Danny pleaded aghast, "I'll be all right on my own."

"Now don't make things difficult, Danny," his father patted his shoulder, and Danny nodded miserably.

Fighting back the tears, the boy busied himself, carrying dishes to the sink.

Later Danny lay in his bed listening. He heard the old lady knock the front door, and Dad's voice as he showed her in.

Danny heard the television switched on. Then the car door slammed, the engine revved and rumbled into the distance.

He shut his eyes tight and decided to pretend that it was really Mum downstairs. He had almost succeeded when a cracked voice squeaked up from the hall.

"You all right, boy?"

Danny lay rigid, afraid she would come up the stairs.

"Yes, Mrs Blewitt," he managed to call back.

"Goodnight boy!" she croaked as she returned to the television.

Danny knew the old woman would be wearing her hat. She had never been seen without a hat. It hid her bald head, the school children whispered.

Everyone knew she was a witch.

CHAPTER TWO

When Danny set off for school next morning the milkman was clanking his way round the council estate. Danny glanced at old Mrs Blewitt's house as he hurried passed. He was surprised to see three bottles of milk on her door-step.

After school Danny stopped as usual at Mrs Blewitt's gate to stroke the large black cat. But Blackie Blewitt was not there.

By the weekend Gran was better and Mum was home again, but Blackie Blewitt had not re-appeared.

Danny took his bike and rode up and down the pavement on his side of the road. Every time he came to Mrs Blewitt's house he slowed down and searched her garden with his eyes. He looked among the untidy spreading shrubs, under the uncut privet hedge, and in the straggly flower beds. But there was no sign of the black cat.

Old Mrs Blewitt came out of her front door, rattling her keys like dry bones. The old woman's

twisted hand in fingerless gloves fumbled with the gate. She swivelled her head on her bent back and Danny felt her bright bird-like eyes pierce him like lasers. Then she bent her head against the wind and shuffled off along the road.

Danny wondered what spells were hidden in the folds of her billowing black coat.

Mum came out to call Danny for lunch. She waved to the old lady as she crossed their road, then said in a low voice as they turned to go indoors, "Off to buy best steak and liver for the cat, and a bit of scrag end of mutton for herself, I shouldn't wonder."

It was several weeks later that Danny first saw Blackie Blewitt again.

He opened his bedroom curtains one morning and looked out. There in Mrs Blewitt's back yard, outside her rickety wooden shed, was the large black cat, sitting washing itself. Around the cat sprawling and rolling on the concrete, was a handful of equally black kittens.

Danny watched their antics in delight. They pounced on each other, and chased each other's tails. They stalked imaginary enemies, and shied sideways at nothing at all. They lay on their backs and wrestled, boxing with tiny black paws. One unwisely pounced on its mother's tail and Mrs Blackie Blewitt dealt it a swift cuff with her big paw. It landed on a heap of its squabbling brothers and sisters.

Danny tried to count how many there were. But they moved so quickly and were so often on top of one another, he couldn't be sure.

Mum called, "Breakfast's ready!" and Danny bounded downstairs to tell her the news.

"Blackie Blewitt's got kittens. Lots of them, all in the back yard."

"I knew there was something going on," said Mum, "All that extra milk, and trips to the butchers."

"She won't be able to keep them," came Dad's voice from behind the newspaper.

"Council won't stand for it," agreed Mum.

"What will happen to them?" asked Danny.

"Council man will come and have them put down," said Mum.

Danny knew that phrase. He'd heard it on television when they talked about stray dogs, but he wanted to be sure of his facts.

"You mean the kittens will have to die?" he questioned.

Both his parents nodded.

CHAPTER THREE

Danny thought about Blackie Blewitt's family all day. On his way home from school, he paused outside old Mrs Blewitt's house. He longed to be in her back yard playing with the black kittens. Perhaps he'd even be able to hold one. He shut his eyes imagining the soft little body in his hand. As he opened his eyes he saw the curtains move and knew the old lady could see him.

He sighed and walked slowly down his own front path. He knew he wouldn't dare to knock Mrs Blewitt's door to ask. Danny sniffed and wondered why he didn't feel like running at full speed into the kitchen.

The next morning the kittens were enjoying their rough and tumble again outside the shed while their mother supervised her children's playtime. Danny was glad to be able to watch them.

He had sniffed and coughed all night and Mum had looked in to say, "No school for you,

my lad. You need a day indoors to shake off
that cold. Stay in bed for now."

Mum had brought his breakfast on a tray, a
real treat, but Danny didn't feel like eating.

He dressed slowly, coughing and spluttering
with the effort. Downstairs Mum ordered him
onto the sofa with a pile of books and comics.
Mum announced that she had to go to the shops
and left Danny with a glass of fruit juice and
strict instructions not to answer the door.

Danny flicked through the comics. He'd read them all. The house was very quiet. Danny was just going to switch on the television to see if there was a cartoon when he heard a strange cry. It came again, almost like a baby, just outside the back window.

The third time Danny recognised the sound, not a baby but a kitten. He looked out and there wandering and stumbling on the path was a very lost kitten.

Danny went outside. With great care he lifted the black bundle of fur and cradled it against his jumper. It mewed pathetically. Danny looked at the bottom of the lap-wood fence and spied a tiny hole. He put the kitten beside the gap but the kitten obstinately refused to go through. Danny was afraid he would hurt it on the jagged wood if he pushed it.

The thought flashed through Danny's mind that he could keep the kitten and hide it. But he dismissed the idea as impossible to carry out and unkind to Mrs Blewitt.

He went back into the house and lifted the kitten to his cheek. He felt the soft warm fur against his skin. Looking into its face he noticed it had a tiny star of white hairs on its forehead.

"I'll have to take you back, won't I?" Danny whispered into its ear.

The kitten mewed and wriggled.

"You can be my lucky charm and protect me from the witch," said Danny. He left the front door ajar and tucked the kitten under his jumper.

CHAPTER FOUR

Danny walked up Mrs Blewitt's front path, took deep breath, and banged the door knocker. The noise echoed, followed by the sound of shuffling feet.

A croaky voice called, "Coming, coming. Who is it?"

The door opened a crack.

Danny swallowed and spoke quickly. "One of the kittens came through the fence. I've bought it back." And he held out the wriggling kitten.

Mrs Blewitt opened the door wider.

"You are a good boy," she squeaked, "bring it in."

Danny hesitated.

"Come in, boy!"

Danny stepped inside. A warm stale smell of cats and old stews enveloped him. The house seemed dark and mostly brown. Danny followed

the old woman through her kitchen where a saucepan bubbled and steamed on the cooker.

At the back door Mrs Blewitt called, "Blackie, Blackie, come and take your lost child."

The big cat appeared.

"Put the kitten down," instructed Mrs Blewitt.

Danny put the kitten at his feet where it squirmed and mewed for a second before its mother picked it up firmly in her mouth and stalked off to the garden shed. Danny watched amazed.

"Doesn't it hurt the kitten, being carried by the neck in its mother's mouth?" he blurted out nasally.

"Not at all," Mrs Blewitt assured him. "Come and see the family."

Danny went into the dark shed. As his eyes became accustomed to the gloom he saw a box half covered with old sacking, on a tin trunk. Inside the box was Mrs Blackie Blewitt and all her family.

"How many kittens? asked Danny.

"Five," replied Mrs Blewitt.

Danny looked in silence, then putting his hand out to stroke Blackie, he asked the question that was aching inside him.

"What does the council man say?"

Mrs Blewitt's twisted hand shot out and grabbed Danny by the shoulder. He felt her crooked fingers holding him like a claw.

"Little busy-body," she hissed. "Going to tell tales are you? People saying they ought to be put down, are they?"

She pushed him angrily towards the house.

"I won't let the council man in. Cats are clean things. Don't do any harm, do they?"

Danny was frightened by her sudden anger, and hurried through the house. But at the door, the thought of the family of kittens gave him the courage to stop and say, "I only meant, can't you find homes for them before the council man comes?"

"Huh!" The old lady's temper evaporated in a sigh.

"Kind homes, that's what they need," she agreed. "I don't know anyone who wants a kitten and I can't afford all the extra food much longer."

Danny ran home, and was back on the sofa with his old comics before his mother returned from the shops.

CHAPTER FIVE

The following week Danny had won his battle with the coughs and sneezes and he had had plenty of time to plan his campaign to save the kittens. At breakfast he tried plan number one.

"The kittens are playing in their yard again," he informed his parents. "I wish I could have one. Could I Mum?"

"No, Danny!" said his mother decisively, "Kittens grow into cats. You'd soon be tired of it and I'd be left feeding it and letting it out. It would just be a nuisance."

"Wretched cats scratch up my seed beds," added Dad.

Danny sighed, he wasn't really surprised, but that was plan number one down the drain.

At school, when the bell rang for play-time Danny hung back. The rest of the class filed out of the class-room. Danny waited for his teacher to notice him, to put plan number two into action.

"Well, Danny?" Mrs Hill looked up from her desk.

"Blackie Blewitt has five kittens," he began, "and they need homes because old Mrs Blewitt can't afford the extra food."

"That is a problem," agreed Mrs Hill, frowning over the top of her spectacles.

"Could you ask the class if anyone wants a kitten?" suggested Danny, emboldened by Mrs Hill's sympathy, "because the council man might come soon and have them put down."

"I'll ask the children," Mrs Hill promised, "Now, out to play, Danny".

Mrs Hill was as good as her word. At the end of the day when the chairs were neatly placed under the desks, the children sat on the rug in the book corner. Mrs Hill read a story about a stray cat that longed for a cosy home. Then she said, "Danny knows some kittens who need homes. Tell us about them, Danny."

Danny blushed crimson.

"Mrs Blewitt's cat has five kittens," he explained. "They're all black and love to play. And the council man might come to take them away," he finished in a rush.

The bell rang for home-time and Danny joined the crush in the cloakroom to extract his anorak. Then he ran home.

The next morning Dad was missing at the breakfast table.

His newspaper lay unopened.

"Where's Dad?" queried Danny.

Mum evaded the question.

"Eat your breakfast before its cold."

Dad passed the kitchen window with a bundle of old newspaper which he was holding gingerly. Mum was busy at the cooker so Danny slid off his chair for closer look through the window. Dad had taken his spade from the shed. He went up the garden to the vegetable patch and began to dig a hole.

"Danny!" his mother said sharply, "Sit on your chair and eat your breakfast."

"But what's Dad doing?" Danny pleaded.

"Never mind, now," Mum replied firmly.

Dad returned to the kitchen. He stood at the sink washing and scrubbing his hands in a bowl of steaming water.

"I'd better go and tell the old lady," he said.

Mum nodded.

Dad eventually took his place at the break-fast table. Danny tried again to discover the reason for such a strange ritual before breakfast.

"Is it the kittens?" he guessed.

"I'm afraid so, son," said his father. "One of them was dead on the pavement this morning. It could have been a dog savaged it, or a car ran over it."

So that was what was in the newspaper bundle now buried in the garden. Danny remembered the soft furry little body he had carried next door. He felt a lump in his throat and he hoped it wasn't that kitten with the tiny white star.

"How can we find homes for them?" he demanded.

"It's not really our problem, Danny," said his father. "The council will deal with them."

"I want to find homes for them before the council man comes, or anymore are lost or killed," said Danny determinedly.

Dad joked, "You'll need an advertising campaign."

CHAPTER SIX

It was when Mrs Hill announced to the class that they would be painting that afternoon, that Danny thought of plan number three.

When the sheets of sugar paper and paint had been given out, Danny asked for an extra pot of black. Ignoring the chatter around him, he became absorbed in his task.

Mrs Hill, looking over Danny's shoulder, recognised his subject at once.

"Is that the family of kittens, Danny?"

Danny nodded, his tongue between his lips, as he concentrated on the bright green eyes.

"One was killed last night," he said dolefully.

When Mrs Hill looked again the four kittens were complete.

"Shall we hang it, Danny?"

Danny shook his head and waited until the teacher had turned her attention to another child.

Then he took a thin brush and some bright red paint. Painting the kittens had been easy compared with this part of the job. His wrist ached by the time he had finished. He stepped back and viewed his work with satisfaction. The letters were a little wobbly but the words were clear —

THESE KITTENS NEED HOMES

Mrs Hill returned.

"Its a poster," Danny explained.

His teacher chuckled. "I think we should put it on the outside of the class-room door. Then everyone will read it."

Danny was pleased.

On the way home from school Danny paused at Mrs Blewitt's gate. One of the kittens was playing on her garden path, chasing rose petals that were being whisked around by the breeze. The kitten noticed Danny and came towards him, mewing.

"Oh no!" Danny groaned. He knew it would find its way onto the road like the other one that was killed. He would have to knock Mrs Blewitt's door. He remembered her claw-like grip on his shoulder and shuddered.

Danny looked up, and in the same instant that he saw the old net curtain twitch, he also saw a stocky red-faced man coming down the road. Danny gasped. It was the council rentman. Of course, it was Thursday, the rentman's day.

The man, draped in his stained overcoat, his surly face squashed beneath a shapeless trilby hat, turned into Danny's house.

Danny reached his arm between the bars of Mrs Blewitt's gate, grabbed the kitten, and stuffed it inside his anorak. It wriggled, and then mercifully lay quiet and still. But the old lady had seen. As Danny stood up she appeared at her front door.

"Here, boy!" she shrieked, "I saw you, pinching things that don't belong to you."

As she came towards him, her black hat tilted forward, Danny stepped backwards and collided with the rentman, who grabbed him by the ear.

"Pesky kids," the man growled. "What were you doing, my lad?"

"Nothing," Danny stammered.

Mrs Blewitt took hold of his shoulder. One bird-like eye winked meaningfully at Danny, letting him know that she now understood the situation.

"I'll tell his mother," she squeaked. "You leave him to me."

"I hope he gets the hiding he deserves," said the council rentman.

"Rent's on the hall table, same as usual," said the old lady, and the rentman stomped off to fetch it.

"Kids and animals," he muttered as he passed them at the garden gate, "I'd ban the lot of them, nothing but trouble, I say."

Mrs Blewitt and Danny stood motionless until he was out of sight in the next house.

"Come in, quickly, boy," the old lady whispered.

Danny ran into her house, relieved that she now knew why he had snatched the kitten.

He gently emptied the warm bundle out of his anorak onto a chair. The kitten looked up at its rescuer.

"It's the one with the star," observed Danny.

"The only one with any marking," said Mrs Blewitt, "And it's always in trouble." She sighed sadly, "I can't keep them any longer. They need homes of their own."

"I'm working on it," Danny assured her.

But Mrs Blewitt just shook her old head distractedly, looking more bent than ever.

Danny ran home.

CHAPTER SIX

"May I have an envelope, Mum?" Danny asked, and then disappeared into his bedroom to put plan number four into action. He took a felt tip pen and sat staring at the blank envelope, sucking the end of the pen. Slowly he began to write.

When he had finished, he folded the envelope, tucked it into his trouser pocket, and ran downstairs.

"Mum," he called, "can I go to the corner shop?"

"No sweets before tea," his mother answered.

"No, Mum," he agreed. He jogged down the path and along the pavement to the main road where the small general stores was situated.

Danny pushed open the door and felt relieved that the shop wasn't busy. The shop lady knew Danny.

"What do you want, lad?"

Danny pulled the envelope from his pocket, and indicated one side of the shop window which was full of postcards of items for sale or wanted.

"Please will you put this in your window?" he asked.

The lady took it and read:-

Black kittens need kind homes
Mrs Blewitt, 5 Blossom Road.

She nodded, "It can go in for a week for ten pence."

Danny put his hand to his mouth. He hadn't thought it would cost money.

"I'll just run home and fetch it," he said.

In his bedroom Danny emptied his money box. A pile of coppers tumbled out. He counted ten pence. Only two pence remained. He'd have to go without sweets until next pocket money day.

By the time he returned to the shop, his envelope was stuck in the window. He hoped someone wanting a kitten would read it.

At school next day, little Jill who had just started school that term, came up to Danny in the play-ground.

"My Mummy says I can have one of those kittens you painted," she announced. Danny could have hugged her, but big boys didn't do that sort of thing in the play-ground.

On the way home, Danny saw little Jill and her mother go into Mrs Blewitt's house carrying a whicker cat basket.

"You've been busy with your advertising campaign," his mother joked as he went into the kitchen. Danny looked at her enquiringly.

"A lady went to Mrs Blewitt's and took a kitten this morning, said she'd read the ad in the shop window."

"Was she nice?" Danny wanted to know.

"Seemed very friendly," said his mother. "Stood talking cats with old Mrs Blewitt at her gate for ages."

"Two to go!" thought Danny.

No-one else arrived that weekend to answer the advertisement. But on Monday Mrs Hill surprised Danny by announcing that she would walk home with him. He noticed a large shopping basket on her desk.

As they walked she explained that she had decided to take a kitten herself.

"My old mother lives with me now," explained Mrs Hill. "She can't go out and she's lonely when I'm out all day. A cat would be lovely company for her."

Danny skipped into his house and told his mother the good news.

"Only one to go," Danny said.

"Hmm!" said his mother, pursing her lips, not seeming to have anything to say on the subject.

Danny did a war-dance round the kitchen. His campaign was going well and tomorrow would be a great day. It was his birthday.

Danny woke early and found a small pile of presents on his bed. He opened them eagerly – a book from Gran, a jigsaw from an Auntie, a construction kit from his cousins; nice but not very exciting. However, he wasn't worried. Last year his big present had been his bike and it had been waiting for him in the kitchen. Thinking of this, he dressed hurriedly and dashed downstairs.

Mum greeted him with a birthday hug and a kiss. Danny gazed round the kitchen, no surprises, and no Dad to greet him. Danny suddenly felt a bit empty inside. Mum seemed too busy at the cooker to notice.

There was a sharp knock on the back door. Danny ran to open it.

"Happy Birthday, son!" Dad strode in with a whicker cat bed, which he laid on the floor revealing the black kitten on the cushion inside.

"For me?" Danny questioned in disbelief.

"For you," affirmed Mum, "but you look after him," she added.

"I will, Mum," he promised. "Of course I'll look after my own kitten."

Danny picked up the wriggling bundle of black fur and looked into its bright green eyes. He felt even happier when he noticed the faint white star on its forehead.

"I'll call him Lucky."

Danny raced home after school to be with his kitten. But he paused at Mrs Blewitt's gate when he noticed the fat black cat in her old place. He bent to stroke her.

Danny looked up as the faded net curtain was pulled aside. This time old Mrs Blewitt waved. Danny grinned and waved back. Then he ran home to Blackie Blewitt's naughtiest and luckiest kitten.